My Bum is SO NOISY!

Dawn McMillan

Illustrated by Ross Kinnaird

SCHOLASTIC

My bum is so noisy.

My bum brings me shame.

It makes **weird** noises and I get the blame.

My bum behaves in a most disorderly way.
Such bad manners when folk come to stay.

It makes a phone **ringing**, sweet sounds of singing. We hear whistling and chirping and **burping** and slurping.

And ...

Popping and squeaking when Auntie is speaking!
Then a **crash** and a **boom** and ...
Uncle leaves the room.

My cousins, though, four of them boys,
all want a bum that makes lots of **noise**.
And while they try hard it seems very strange
that each of their bums has a limited range.

Not a horn-blowing boat, not a musical note …
No snorting, no snoring – my cousins are boring.
But … my bum makes sounds beyond belief!

And …

My cousins are failures, to Auntie's relief.

Poor Mum and Dad – what can they say
about having a son that behaves in this way?
They breathe and they sigh, but they hold their
heads high.

And ...

Amid all the stares, the fuss and the tiz,
they say,

'He's our boy and
he's fine as he is.'

But **I need a new bum!** A bum that is quiet.
A bum that is good and won't cause a riot.
A bum that doesn't go **honk** in the park.
A bum that won't scare the dogs with a **bark**.

No **slapping**, no clapping, no rapping or napping.

No blipping, no **banging**, no clinking, no **clanging**.

But wait ...

Somebody is coming! Somebody is running ...
And then I hear ... so **loud** and so clear ...

'We've found him! He's perfect! Just what we need.
We'll sign him at once, when all is agreed!'

And now...

My bum's in the movies. I am SO proud.
My bum makes the noises, gentle and loud.
Just the right noises to go with the story ...

Like...
BIG booming
explosions
to go with the glory.

All my hooting and hollering has quite a following.

I do **splishes** and splashes,

collisions and **crashes.**

Each cough and each sneeze.

All the wind in the trees, the sound of **tornadoes**,

the **swarming** of bees.

All the waves **rolling** in,
all the **thunder** and din.
Yes, my bum is the greatest.
And, here is the latest ...

My bum is famous! I'm known worldwide!
I have the **loudest**,
the proudest ...
the most uproarious,
Victorious ...

Sound-system backside!

About the author

Hi, I'm Dawn McMillan. I'm from Waiomu, a small coastal village on the western side of the Coromandel Peninsula in New Zealand. I live with my husband Derek and our cat, Lola. I work from a small studio in my back garden, with a view of the sea. I write some sensible stories and lots of crazy stories. I had fun writing this latest crazy story and hope you have fun with it too.

About the illustrator

Hi. I'm Ross. I love to draw. When I'm not drawing, or being cross with my computer, I love most things involving the sea and nature. I also work from a little studio in my garden surrounded by birds and trees. I live in Auckland, New Zealand. I hope you like reading this book as much as I enjoyed illustrating it.

This edition published in the UK by Scholastic, 2021
Euston House, 24 Eversholt Street, London, NW1 1DB
Scholastic Ireland, 89E Lagan Road, Dublin Industrial Estate, Glasnevin, Dublin, D11 HP5F
First published in Australia and New Zealand by Oratia Media, 2021

Text © Dawn McMillan, 2021
Illustrations © Ross Kinnaird, 2021
The moral rights of Dawn McMillan and Ross Kinnaird have been asserted.

ISBN 978 07023 0594 8

10 9 8 7

www.scholastic.co.uk